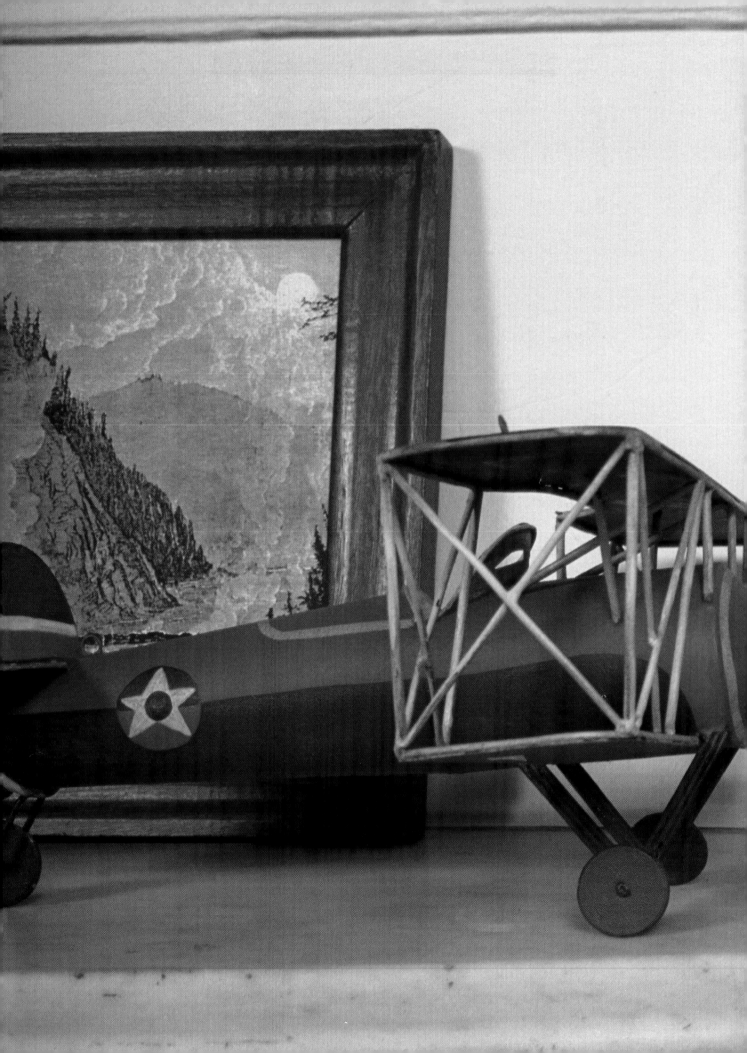

You Are Here
Nina Crews

Greenwillow Books, New York

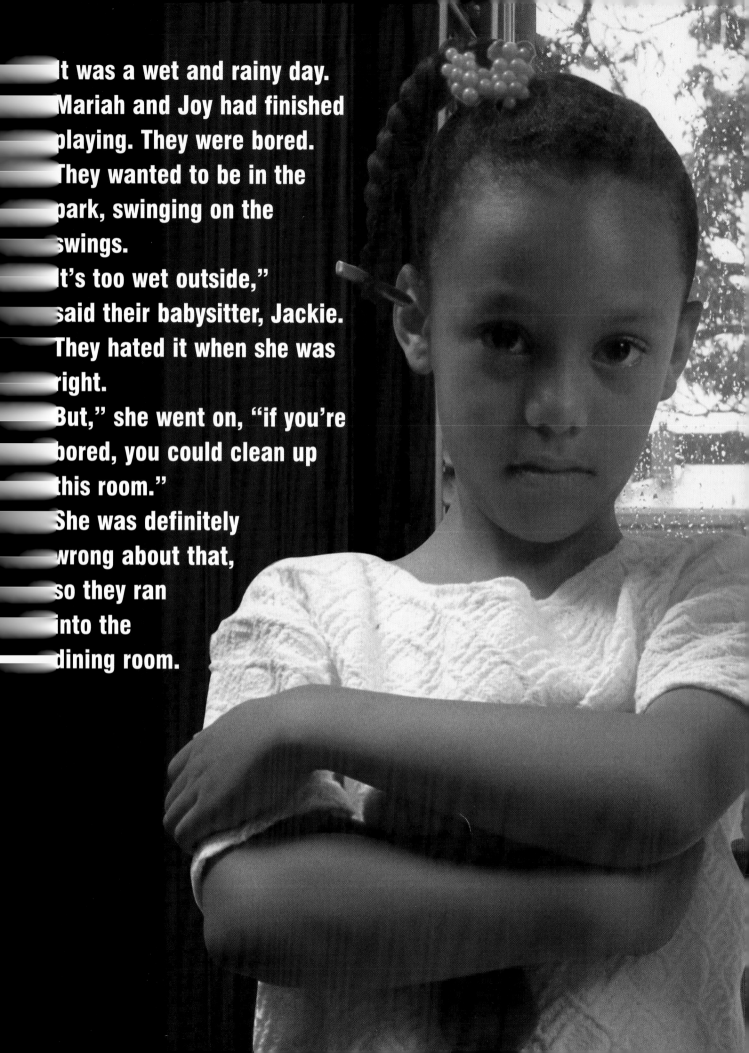

It was a wet and rainy day. Mariah and Joy had finished playing. They were bored. They wanted to be in the park, swinging on the swings.

It's too wet outside," said their babysitter, Jackie. They hated it when she was right.

But," she went on, "if you're bored, you could clean up this room." She was definitely wrong about that, so they ran into the dining room.

Joy had an idea. "I know. We'll take a trip."

Mariah said, "Okay. We'll need a map."

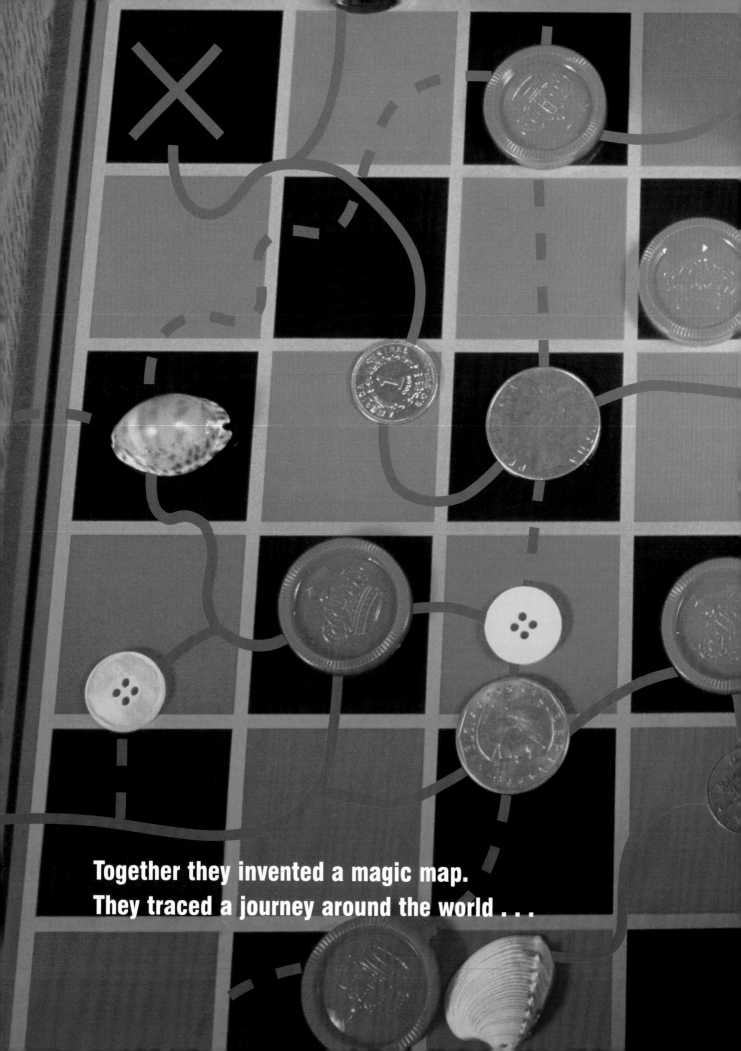

Together they invented a magic map.
They traced a journey around the world . . .

and they flew far, far away.

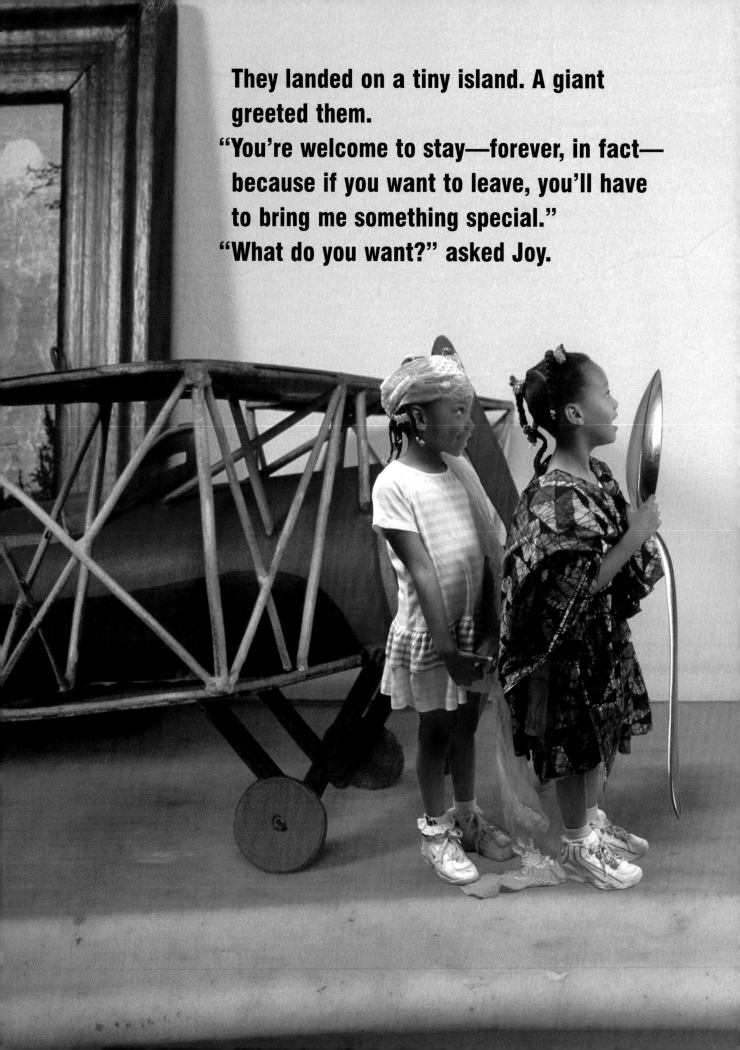

They landed on a tiny island. A giant greeted them.
"You're welcome to stay—forever, in fact—because if you want to leave, you'll have to bring me something special."
"What do you want?" asked Joy.

"This island is filled with treasures,"
said the giant.
"Where?" asked Mariah.
"Follow your map," said the giant.

Before long they found themselves in a jungle. A penguin appeared, then shuffled off through the palms. They followed him.

He led them to the lair of a fierce monster,
who was guarding many treasures.
"Could we have a jewel to give the giant?"
asked Mariah.
The creature narrowed its eyes and hissed.
"What will we do?" cried Joy.

They looked at their map.
"The sorcerer's library! We can find
a book of magic spells," said Mariah.

They danced and chanted a spell outside the monster's lair. The beast fell asleep immediately.

Unfortunately, the monster was lying on top of the treasures.

All they could do was sit and wait.

When it woke up, the
monster purred. The spell
had made it much friendlier.

**Mariah and Joy traded their shield
for a multicolored jewel.
"Now let's go home," said Joy.**

They headed toward their plane, but somehow they
took a wrong turn. They were in a deep, dark forest.
"I think we're lost," said Mariah.
"Why don't we use our map?" said Joy.

"But everything's
spinning!"
said Mariah.
She started to giggle.
"This is a crazy map,"
screeched Joy.
"Where's the giant?
Where's the monster?"

"Where are we?" they cried.

"You are here," said their mother. "What are you girls doing? Jackie said that you've been playing in here for ages. The sun is out. Let's go to the park."

"We won't need
a map this time,"
said Joy.
"We know the way."

MARIAH CREWS as Mariah
JOY HENRY as Joy
DONNA CREWS as their mother
COSMO CREWS as the monster
Thanks to all of you. You were terrific.

Thanks to Mike Turoff for his many hours
of computer advice and assistance.
Thanks also to family and friends, whose
support and comments are always welcome.

The full-color photo collages were created digitally using Adobe Photoshop™.   The text type is Swiss 721 Black Condensed BT.   Copyright © 1998 by Nina Crews.   All rights reserved. No part of this book may be reproduced or utilized in any form or by any means, electronic or mechanical, including photocopying, recording, or by any information storage and retrieval system, without permission in writing from the Publisher, Greenwillow Books, a division of William Morrow & Company, Inc., 1350 Avenue of the Americas, New York, NY 10019.   www.williammorrow.com   Printed in Hong Kong by South China Printing Company (1988) Ltd.   First Edition 10 9 8 7 6 5 4 3 2 1
Library of Congress Cataloging-in-Publication Data: Crews, Nina. You are here / by Nina Crews.   p.   cm.   Summary: When the rain keeps Mariah and Joy confined to the indoors, they create a magic map and go on a fantastic imaginary voyage.   ISBN 0-688-15753-X (trade).   ISBN 0-688-15754-8 (lib. bdg.)   [1. Imagination—Fiction.   2. Voyages and travels—Fiction.   3. Afro-Americans—Fiction.]   I. Title.   PZ7.C8683Yo 1998 [E]—dc21 97-36312 CIP AC